MUCUS ATTACK!

Ready, Set, Science!
Read all these fabulous, fact-filled, *funny*
MAD SCIENCE® books:

#1 What a Blast!
The Explosive Escapades of
Ethan Flask and Professor von Offel

#2 Now You See It . . .
The Incredible Illusions of
Ethan Flask and Professor von Offel

#3 Mucus Attack!
The Icky Investigations of
Ethan Flask and Professor von Offel

MUCUS ATTACK!

The Icky Investigations of
Ethan Flask and Professor von Offel

MAD SCIENCE

by Kathy Burkett
Creative development by Gordon Korman

SCHOLASTIC INC.

New York   Toronto   London   Auckland   Sydney
Mexico City   New Delhi   Hong Kong   Buenos Aires

No part of this publication may be reproduced in whole or in part, or stored in a retrieval system or transmitted in any form or by any means, electronic, mechanical, photocopying, recording, or otherwise, without written permission of the Mad Science Group, 3400 Jean-Talon W., Suite 101, Montreal, Quebec H3R 2E8

0-439-20725-8

Library of Congress Cataloging-in-Publication Data available

12 11 10 9 8 7 6 5 4 3 2 1   2 3 4 5 6 7/0
                                                      40
Printed in the U.S.A.

Table of Contents

Prologue

For more than a hundred years, the Flasks, the town of Arcana's first family of science, have been methodically, precisely, safely — in other words, scientifically — inventing all kinds of things.

For more than a hundred years, the von Offels, Arcana's first family of sneaks, have been stealing those inventions.

Where the Flasks are brilliant, rational, and reliable, the von Offels are brilliant, reckless, and ruthless. The nearly fabulous Flasks could have earned themselves a major chapter in the history of science — but at every key moment, there always seemed to be a von Offel on the scene to "borrow" a science notebook, beat a Flask to the punch on a patent, or booby-trap an important experiment. Just take a look at the Flask family tree and then at the von Offel clan's tree. Coincidence? Or evidence!

Despite being tricked out of fame and fortune by the awful von Offels, the Flasks have doggedly continued their scientific inquiries. The last of the family line, Ethan Flask, is no exception. An outstanding sixth-grade science teacher, he's also conducting studies into animal intelligence and is competing for the Third Millennium Foundation's prestigious Vanguard Teacher Award. Unfortunately, the person who's evaluating Ethan for the award is none other than Professor John von Offel, a.k.a. the original mad scientist, Johannes von Offel.

Von Offel needs a Flask to help him regain the body he lost in an explosive experiment many decades ago. So far, the professor's attempts have only created chaos. He had everybody at Einstein Elementary seeing things in Now You See It . . . The Incredible Illusions of Ethan Flask and Professor von Offel —

including an orangutan who saw von Offel as his perfect mate!

But this time, the professor vows things will be different. After all, isn't Ethan Flask going to do a unit on the human body?

Just what the professor needs. A fully human body!

The Nearly-Fabulous Flasks

Jedidiah Flask
2nd person to create rubber band

Oliver Flask
Missed appointment to patent new glue because he was mysteriously epoxied to his chair

Augustus Flask
Developed telephone; got a busy signal

Mildred Flask Tachyon
Tranquilizer formula never registered; carriage horses fell asleep en route to patent office

Lane Tachyon
Developed laughing gas; was kept in hysterics while a burglar stole the formula

Percy Flask
Lost notes on cure for common cold in pick-pocketing incident

Archibald Flask
Knocked out cold en route to patent superior baseball bat

Marlow Flask
Runner-up to Adolphus von Offel for Sir Isaac Newton Science Prize

Amaryllis Flask Lepton
Discovered new kind of amoeba; never published findings due to dysentery

Norton Flask
Clubbed with seven-minute gray meat loaf and robbed of prototype microwave oven

Salome Flask Rhombus
Discovered cloud-salting with dry ice; never made it to patent office due to freak downpour

Roland Flask
His new high-speed engine was believed to have powered the getaway car that stole his prototype

Constance Rhombus Ampère
Lost Marie Curie Award to Beatrice O'Door; voted Miss Congeniality

Margaret Flask Geiger
Name was mysteriously deleted from registration papers for her undetectable correction fluid

Michael Flask
Arrived with gas grill schematic only to find tailgate party outside patent office

Solomon Ampère
Bionic horse placed in Kentucky Derby after von Offel entry

Ethan Flask

The Awful von Offels

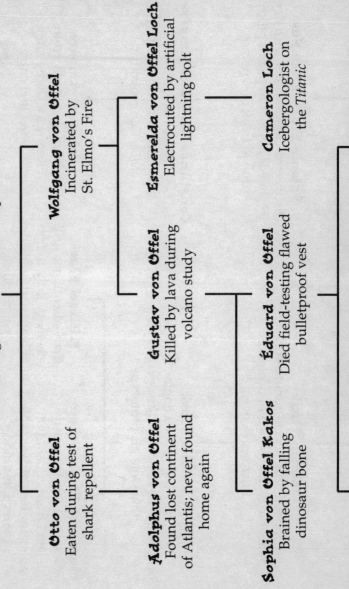

Johannes von Offel
Died creating the world's safest explosive

Wolfgang von Offel
Incinerated by
St. Elmo's Fire

Otto von Offel
Eaten during test of
shark repellent

Esmerelda von Offel Loch
Electrocuted by artificial
lightning bolt

Gustav von Offel
Killed by lava during
volcano study

Adolphus von Offel
Found lost continent
of Atlantis; never found
home again

Cameron Loch
Icebergologist on
the *Titanic*

Eduard von Offel
Died field-testing flawed
bulletproof vest

Sophia von Offel Kakos
Brained by falling
dinosaur bone

Rula von Offel Malle
Evaporated

Beatrice Malle O'Door
Drowned pursuing the
Loch Ness Monster

Feldspar O'Door
Died of freezer burn
during cryogenics
experiment

Kurt von Offel
Weak batteries in
antigravity backpack

Colin von Offel
Transplanted his brain
into wildebeest

Alan von Offel
Failed to survive field
test of nonpoisonous
arsenic

Felicity von Offel Day
Brained by diving bell
during deep-sea
exploration

Professor John von Offel (?)

Johannes von Offel's
Book of Scientific Observations,
1891

I am writing this entry from my hospital bed. I now realize that I used too much nitroglycerine in my eternal life draught. The doctor informs me that I blew nearly three millimeters off the tip of my nose, but I'm not sure I trust that charlatan. Speaking of charlatans, Jedidiah Flask is studying the effects of physical exercise on health and life span. The poor fool actually seems to believe that hard work, and not a quick fix, will make the human body last longer. What utter claptrap! But just in case there's some wisdom to his foolishness, I've had my parrot, Atom, fly in his open window to steal his experiment notes.

CHAPTER 1

One A-maze-ing Mouse

Prescott Forrester III stood shivering in the parking lot of Einstein Elementary School. He squinted into the rosy sunrise, then dug his hands deeper into his pockets and yawned. A lone headlight appeared at the end of the street. Prescott rubbed his eyes. Was his mind playing tricks on him? He thought he saw someone on a bike pulling a very large pizza behind him. Maybe if he had

1

eaten a bigger breakfast he wouldn't be imagining enormous pizzas.

"Good morning, Prescott!" The bike rider pulled up to the school and removed his helmet. Prescott smiled. It was his sixth-grade science teacher, Mr. Flask.

"Thanks for coming. I can always use help with animal care in the morning," Mr. Flask said.

"I like feeding our classroom pets," Prescott replied. "Of course, the extra credit you offered didn't hurt."

Mr. Flask locked up his bike and untied the cords that held down a large, flat cardboard box. Prescott helped his teacher lift it. They headed up the school steps.

The box was light but hard to handle because of its size. "I guess there's no pizza in here," Prescott said. "This box feels empty."

"It's not *exactly* empty," said Mr. Flask. He was interrupted by two loud voices.

"Looks like we made it just in time!" Alberta

Wong and Luis Antilla ran up the steps behind them.

"Great!" said Mr. Flask. "Everybody grab a side. I'll go unload the rest of the things off my bike."

The lab assistants neared the front doors of the school. Prescott balanced his side of the box against the door while they waited for Mr. Flask.

Bam! Bam! Bam! Someone pounded on the doors from the inside. Suddenly, the doors flew open. Mr. Klumpp, the school custodian, stood there dour-faced, with his arms crossed.

"Blocking the front door is a fire code violation," he barked.

"We're sorry," Alberta said. "It's so early. We didn't know anyone would be inside already."

"Of course, I'm here early!" Mr. Klumpp shook his head. "Nobody understands a custodian's job, the sacrifices we make."

Mr. Flask bounded up the stairs carrying a cage. "Good morning, Mr. Klumpp!" he called.

The custodian grunted. "Another animal, I see. That's one more cage to clean."

"Leave that to my trusty lab assistants," Ethan replied.

Mr. Klumpp looked at them skeptically. "We'll see," he said. "I'll be checking their work, of course." With a scowl on his face, he stepped aside to let them pass.

"Put that box over by the window," Mr. Flask said when they all reached the science lab. "Then come meet Wendy, the newest member of our classroom." He set the cage he'd been carrying on his desk, opened its door, and placed his hand in front of it. A white mouse stepped out onto his palm and cautiously sniffed around.

"She's cute," Prescott said. "Is she looking for food? I think Sean Baxter dropped some cheese puffs during class yesterday. Maybe Mr. Klumpp missed one when he was mopping."

Mr. Flask laughed. "Mr. Klumpp never misses a thing! Besides, Wendy is in training, and her menu doesn't include leftover junk food."

"What's she training for?" Alberta asked.

"Wendy is part of my latest experiment," Mr. Flask replied. He handed the little white mouse to Prescott. She immediately ran up his arm and tried to duck inside his collar. Prescott grabbed her and gently cupped the mouse in his hands. Meanwhile, Mr. Flask lifted the lid of the large, flat box. Inside were dozens of cardboard walls that formed narrow, twisting paths.

"A maze?" Luis asked.

Mr. Flask nodded. "There are more than a hundred feet of track winding around in there, with a dozen dead ends. To run this maze quickly, a mouse has to be in both good physical and good mental shape."

"Cool," Alberta said. "Did you make this maze yourself?"

"With some help from my 19th-century ancestor, Jedidiah Flask," Mr. Flask said. "I copied this maze design from one of his science notebooks. He was interested in the effects of exercise on the body and the brain. I decided to continue his work, using Wendy."

Prescott opened one hand to give Wendy a clear view of the large, winding maze. "I hope you're feeling frisky, girl."

"I want to find out how regular exercise and a healthy diet affect Wendy's maze time," Mr. Flask continued. "My hypothesis is that she'll have a stronger body and a sharper mind — and so a faster maze time."

Mr. Flask unwrapped a chunk of cheese and placed it in one corner of the racecourse. "The finish line," he explained. Wendy stood up on her hind legs, apparently smelling the cheese. Her whiskers twitched in the air.

Mr. Flask pulled a stopwatch out of his pocket. "Prescott, when I say 'go,' put Wendy in that far corner. That's the starting block."

"But why would you test her before she's even followed your exercise program?" Prescott asked. Wendy made another break for

Prescott's collar. He caught her just before she slipped down his shirt.

"Control," Luis said.

"I'm controlling her the best I can!" Prescott said. "But this mouse seems to think she can walk all over me." Wendy ran up Prescott's sleeve again, skirted his neck, then ran down his other sleeve and sat on his palm. Prescott grinned and shrugged. "I guess she *can* walk all over me."

"No, I meant that this first maze run would be a control trial," Luis explained. "It'll show how fast Wendy runs now. Then, when Mr. Flask times her after her special training regimen, he'll know whether she's improved or not."

"Oh, I see." Prescott held Wendy over the starting block.

"Ready, set . . . go!" Mr. Flask clicked the stopwatch as Prescott lowered Wendy into the maze. Wendy sniffed around for a moment, then took off running. She wandered down a dead end, then turned around and got back on track. After taking a few more wrong turns and backtracking, the mouse finally made it to the finish line.

As she nibbled her cheese, Mr. Flask checked his stopwatch. "Not bad, but there's definitely room for some improvement. Okay, let's feed all the rest of the animals and get ready for class."

Just before the bell rang, Professor John von Offel walked into the sixth-grade science class. Behind him fluttered his constant companion, a comic-looking parrot named Atom.

"No slipups today," the professor warned Atom. "You're an ordinary pet bird, remember? And I'm an ordinary scientist from an ordinary foundation. I'm just here to evaluate young Flask for the Vanguard Teacher Award."

"At least my body casts a shadow," Atom replied. "If I could accidentally fall *through* my chair, I'd be more worried about myself," the parrot added. The professor looked around at the students and put a little extra effort into appearing solid. Since he had only brought himself 65 percent back to life, he found this to be annoyingly difficult.

Wendy's cage sat on the professor's desk. The mouse ran busily, turning an exercise wheel.

"Hey, someone left me a snack!" Atom hopped from the professor's shoulder onto the desk. Wendy jumped out of her wheel and burrowed under some wood shavings.

Prescott ran back to the professor's desk. "I'm sorry, Professor, I'll move Wendy's cage for you."

As Prescott set the cage between a saltwater aquarium and a lizard habitat, he heard a voice behind him squawk, "Wendy. What a perfect name for fast food." He looked back at the professor, who was pinching Atom's beak shut.

Prescott rushed over to Luis and Alberta. "Wendy's in trouble! I just heard Atom refer to her as 'fast food.'"

"The professor's parrot?" Luis asked. "You must have misunderstood. He was probably just repeating something he heard during lunch period."

"His owner is a ghost who can walk through trains," Prescott replied. "Is it really so weird that his bird can talk in real sentences?"

The bell rang as Mr. Flask was programming a small microwave oven. "A healthy popcorn snack for the newest member of our menagerie," he explained, "butter-free, of course." Prescott held up Wendy's cage for everyone to see. The mouse poked her head out of the shavings.

"Now, before we get started today, I want to remind everybody about the upcoming school costume dance," Mr. Flask began. "I spent the weekend assembling an incredible sound system. It's guaranteed to saturate every inch of the gymnasium with sound, without damaging any eardrums."

Sean raised his hand. "Who's going to pick the music?" he asked.

Mr. Flask shrugged. "Well, Dr. Kepler asked *me* to."

A muffled groan spread through the classroom.

"I have a pretty good CD collection," Mr. Flask said.

Another muffled groan.

"Of course, you're welcome to bring your own dance tunes, too," he added.

Alberta raised her hand. She glanced back at the professor and said loudly, "Mr. Flask, you *are* the best science teacher we've ever had." Then she lowered her voice. "But you are, well, kind of *old* — I mean, over twenty and all. Maybe you should work with an expert."

Mr. Flask laughed. "Okay, I'm open. Who do you suggest?"

"Well, looking at this scientifically," Alberta said, "the best dancers in the class are Sean and Heather."

Heather Patterson tossed her perfect hair. "I'd love to help, Mr. Flask, but I'll be too busy dancing."

"Sean?" Mr. Flask asked.

"Play my favorite tunes?" Sean asked. "Dance on a stage in front of everyone? I'm there!"

The popcorn in the microwave had been steadily popping faster and faster. Its warm smell began to fill the room.

"Pass the popcorn!" Sean called out.

Prescott nodded. "That smell makes my mouth water!"

"Great observation," Mr. Flask said. "Any idea why your body would want to make extra saliva when it senses food?"

"Maybe drooling makes you look so pitiful that people feed you?" Sean suggested.

"Sorry, Sean, the popcorn's not for you," said Mr. Flask. "Anybody else?"

Prescott thought for a moment. "Well, spit, uh, I mean saliva makes food wet. Maybe that makes it easier to eat. Who'd want to swallow dry popcorn?"

"Very good!" Mr. Flask said. "There's something else, too. Anyone?"

Mr. Flask walked to the back of the classroom and pulled a box of saltine crackers out of a cupboard. "I just so happen to have the ingredients for a quick experiment on saliva. Lab assistants, could you pass these crackers out? I'm going to feed Wendy her popcorn."

Sean looked at his cracker critically. "This certainly doesn't look very mouthwatering. Couldn't we experiment with something a little more sugary?"

"Stick with me on this, Sean," Mr. Flask said. "I think you'll be pleasantly surprised."

Luis approached the professor with a cracker. "Would you like to join our experiment, Professor von Offel?"

The professor waved the cracker away.

Luis turned to the parrot. "Atom want a cracker?" The bird scrambled for the whole cracker box. Luis pulled it away. "Sorry, Polly, one per customer."

"Okay, everyone start chewing," Mr. Flask said. "Don't swallow the cracker, though. I'm going to ask you to hold it in your mouth for a few minutes."

The room filled with crunching sounds. They quickly faded away as the crackers grew soggy.

"In the interest of science, I'm going to ask you to talk with your mouth full," Mr. Flask said. "Just try not to spray the person in front of you. Can anyone share some observations?"

Prescott raised his hand. He used his tongue to shove the ground-up cracker into one cheek. "My cracker was superdry at first, but then my mouth made enough spit to wet it."

"Yeah, mine's totally, disgustingly gunky," Max Hoof said. "Can we swallow now?"

Mr. Flask shook his head. "Can anyone tell me what they taste?"

"It's a cracker," Sean said. "I taste salt, what else?"

"Give it a few minutes," Mr. Flask said.

"Swish it around like mouthwash to help mix in your saliva. Try to notice what you're tasting."

After a minute, Alberta raised her hand. "Mine tastes sweet!"

"Hey, mine, too!" Heather said. "But it's still disgusting."

"Okay, you can swallow now," Mr. Flask said.

"Where did that sweet taste come from?" Heather asked. "Was it just a trick, like an optical illusion?"

"Interesting hypothesis, Heather, but what you tasted was real," Mr. Flask answered. "Your saliva is full of chemicals called enzymes. Their job is to begin digesting your food — breaking it into chemicals your body can use. One enzyme, called amylase, took the starch in your cracker and broke it down into a simpler chemical — a sugar called glucose."

Alberta raised her hand. "Okay, we swallowed our crackers, so now the sugar is down in our stomachs. Our bodies turn it into energy somehow, right? But how does the energy get to our muscles?"

"And why does our body turn starch into sugar, anyway?" Max asked. "I thought sugar was bad for you."

Sean rolled up his sleeve and flexed his biceps. "I always knew that was wrong. See, I'm living proof."

"Why not just feed Wendy a spoonful of sugar?" Heather said. "Why go to the trouble of making her popcorn?"

"Great questions!" Mr. Flask said. "There's too much material here to cover today, though. I'd say we've just picked our next science unit — the human body . . . with perhaps a bit on the mouse body as well."

The professor cleared his throat loudly. "Is this what you model your curriculum on, Flask? Snack food for a rodent?"

"Awk, rodent snack food, rodent snack food, awk!" Atom eyed Wendy's cage hungrily. The professor snatched him up and plopped him on top of his perch.

Mr. Flask smiled a little nervously. "Naturally, I cover all of the required material. But as I said in my Vanguard Teacher Award application, I like to follow students' interests."

"Oh?" the professor scoffed. He pointed at Max. "Well, *that* young man's main interest this morning has been removing dried mucus from his nostrils."

Sean laughed loudly. "You've been caught yellow-handed, nose-picker!"

Max frowned stubbornly. "It's not fair! I have a cold!"

The professor boomed on. "Well, Flask, does nose mucus a science curriculum make?" It sounded like a challenge.

Mr. Flask smiled. "I'll see what I can do!" The bell rang.

After class, the professor grabbed Atom and stalked to his office. He slammed the door behind him, then turned to Atom.

"You're supposed to be a simple parrot! Instead, you're drooling over that mouse like a starving man eyeing a rare steak!"

Atom stuck his beak in the air. "Listen, pal, how would you like to spend a hundred years eating nothing but bird seed? While you were dead, they discovered that I may be related to dinosaurs. I may look like the Froot Loops toucan, but I've got the soul of a raptor! I need to hunt!"

The professor scowled. "Just make sure you don't get caught."

Atom flew off in a huff.

CHAPTER 2

Better Living
Through Mucus

Work it, work it, work it," Heather chanted. As she and Alberta waited for science class to begin, they held a tiny rope for Wendy. It was slightly raised. The mouse jumped steadily back and forth over the rope for a few minutes before she finally seemed to tire. The girls encouraged the mouse to jump a few more times, then let her rest.

"Great workout!" Heather said. "You go, girl!"

Alberta rolled her eyes. "It's not like Wendy understands you, Heather."

"Enthusiasm is contagious," Heather said. "That's the number one rule of cheerleading. It applies to most other areas of life as well." Heather pulled a little cage out from under her desk. "To give Wendy even more encouragement, I've brought her a workout partner." She opened the door to the cage, and a light gray mouse poked out its nose warily. "This is Cindy."

"Wendy and Cindy?" Alberta made a face.

Heather smiled. "Cute, isn't it? They'll be like mouse sisters." She put the gray mouse down and dangled the jump rope in front of her. "Okay, get revved up for your turn, Cindy."

Heather and Alberta began to swing the tiny jump rope, but Cindy just crouched down. She flattened her body out so that the rope wouldn't hit her, then she yawned.

"Looks like Cindy's not revved," said Alberta.

Heather stopped swinging the rope. "Maybe she's tired. After all, it was a long journey from my house to science class — a long trip for a mouse, that is. Maybe a healthy snack will revive her."

Alberta fetched the day-old bag of popcorn and poured some onto the table. Wendy picked up a kernel and started nibbling. But Cindy sniffed the bag and turned away.

"Maybe it's stale," Alberta said.

"I know, I have a little fresh fruit salad left over from lunch." Heather opened the container and held it out to the two mice. Wendy balanced her paws on the edge and reached in for a bite of melon. Cindy just turned up her whiskered nose.

Heather frowned. "Cindy must be craving something else healthy, like granola or green veggies. Maybe I better take her home tonight so she can eat dinner. I could bring her back in the morning."

"It's almost time for class to start. We better finish up," Alberta said.

"Mr. Flask says Cindy can spend each school day in Wendy's cage," Heather said. "After all, if they're going to be best friends, these mice need some face time." She carried the two little animals back to Wendy's cage. Atom was perched on the top. "Shoo," Heather commanded. Atom retreated, and Heather slipped the mice into the cage. Then she closed the latch.

The bell rang.

"At the professor's suggestion," Mr. Flask began, "today's opening topic is . . . mucus."

"Excellent," Sean said. "I brought in a visual aid." He held up a beige plastic nose and shook it. "It's full of one of my favorite kinds of candy. See, look!" He opened a little flap where one of the nostrils would be and shook out a yellowish-gray clump of candy.

"Gross!" Heather wrinkled her nose.

"That is pretty realistic," Alberta said.

Sean thrust the nose at Max. "Have some. They taste just like homemade!"

Max pushed the candy away, and a few pieces tumbled to the ground.

"Puh-lease, Mr. Flask," Heather pleaded. "Can't we talk about something less disgusting? I for one could do without mucus."

Mr. Flask smiled. "Actually, Heather, you couldn't. Mucus is a matter of life and death."

The professor raised an eyebrow and began taking notes with his old-fashioned quill pen.

"Let's all take a deep breath." Mr. Flask inhaled a chestful of air and blew it out noisily. "Feel refreshed? Well, air may feel clean, but it's actually full of small particles like dust, pollen, smoke, and germs."

"Ick! Pass the face mask," Heather said.

"Mucus is your body's *natural* face mask," Mr. Flask said. "Mucus is like a filter. Its job is to catch germs and other particles and keep them from reaching your lungs. That's why there's mucus coating most of your respiratory tract. That includes the inside of your nose, your throat, and your *trachea*, the tube leading down to your lungs."

"Then what?" Luis asked. "Does that junk just sit there until I sneeze, cough, or blow my nose?"

"Your body certainly does get rid of old, germy mucus in those ways," Mr. Flask said. "But the main thing that happens to used mucus is — brace yourself — you *swallow* it."

The class groaned. Mr. Flask smiled. "In fact, you may swallow about a quart of mucus a day. That's equal to about two and a half cans of soda."

More groans. A bigger smile from Mr. Flask.

"Doesn't that hurt your stomach?" Alberta asked. "I mean, I feel sick just thinking about it."

"Not at all," Mr. Flask said. "In fact, your stomach already has its own coating of mucus. It has to. The acids in your stomach complete the job your saliva enzymes started. So they have to be strong enough to break down all kinds of food. That means these acids are also strong enough to break down your body tissue. That mucus coating actually saves your stomach from digesting itself."

Alberta smiled. "Better living through mucus!"

"Mucus does other good things for you, too," Mr. Flask continued. "It keeps the inside of your respiratory tract from drying out. It helps your chewed-up lumps of food sliiiiide down your throat. It . . ."

"Mr. Fla-ask!" Max interrupted. "One of the mice is loose." He pointed under Sean's chair.

There was a fluttering sound in the back of the classroom. Prescott whipped his head around in time to catch Atom flying away from the back row of cages.

Sean scrambled up on top of his desk and peered down nervously. "A mouse? Where? What's it doing?"

"I think it's eating the mucus candy you spilled," Max said.

Atom fluttered onto the professor's desk. He craned his neck to see the floor under Sean's desk.

A little gray head peeked out from under Sean's chair, a yellowish-gray chunk in its teeth.

"Cindy!" Heather ran over and snatched her up. "No candy! You're in training! What are you thinking? Put that down!" The gray mouse gulped the chewy chunk and scanned the floor for more.

Sean climbed down from his desk, laughing. "Cindy must have heard Mr. Flask say that mucus is good for you."

Heather carried the gray mouse back to Wendy's cage. The door was open. "I could have sworn I latched the cage," Heather said. She shut Cindy back inside. Wendy was running inside her exercise wheel. Heather tapped on the side of the cage. "That's great, Wendy," she said. "But maybe you could give Cindy a turn." Startled, Wendy hopped off the wheel and burrowed under some wood chips. Cindy walked right past the wheel and curled up lazily in a corner.

Prescott leaned over to Alberta. "I bet that bird unlatched Wendy's cage," he whispered.

Alberta rolled her eyes. "Heather probably forgot to latch the cage. She may look like a goddess, but she makes mistakes like the rest of us mortals."

Prescott shrugged. "I'm still keeping an eye on the bird," he said.

Mr. Flask said, "Okay, everybody, settle down. Let's get to the first experiment of the day. Each lab group needs a fork, three packets of gelatin, and half a cup of hot tap water. Stir the gelatin into the water."

As they stirred, Mr. Flask walked around and added corn syrup to each group's mixture.

Sean pulled out his fork. A gooey strand sagged from the end. "Ugh! Don't tell me — is this mucus?"

The professor sat up straighter in his seat. He adjusted his monocle.

"Great deduction, Sean!" Mr. Flask said. "How did you guess we were making artificial mucus?"

"Well, it's gooey — and it's gross," Sean said.

"Mucus has to be sticky and gooey enough to coat your nose, throat, and stomach, right?" Mr. Flask said. "You haven't even seen gross yet, though." He passed around a baggie of dust and lint for kids to add to their artificial mucus. "Check out what your mucus looks like after it's picked up some particles."

Sean stirred a heaping spoonful of dust and lint into his group's beaker. "This is definitely grosser," he said.

The professor stood up and began walking around the room. He peered into each beaker. "Fascinating, Flask. Is this actually bodily mucus?"

"No, but as you know, the protein from the gelatin and the sugars from the corn syrup share the same primary ingredients as real mucus," Mr. Flask replied.

The professor was standing over Alberta, who was stirring her group's beaker. "May I?" he asked. She handed the beaker to him. Professor von Offel scooped out a long string of goo with his finger and admired it. "Astounding! Did you see this, Atom?"

Alberta looked around. "Uh, Professor, Atom isn't with you."

He looked at her sharply. "Why does that concern you, young lady?"

"It doesn't," Alberta said. "But you just asked him whether he had seen the artificial mucus."

"Nonsense!" The professor frowned. "Why would I ask a common, ordinary bird such a question? Naturally, he couldn't answer me." He started to walk away.

"Professor?" Alberta called after him. "I'm not sure we're done with our mucus."

The professor looked down at the beaker

still in his hand. "Of course," he said. He thrust it at her and walked away.

Alberta turned to Prescott. "The professor is definitely in a world of his own," she said. "But with all this mucus stuff I think Mr. Flask may have finally impressed him. Maybe he can still win the Vanguard Teacher Award after all."

Prescott was looking around for Atom. "I'm less worried about that strange old bird than I am about *his* strange old bird. I wouldn't trust that parrot as far as I could throw him, which is a distance I'd love to measure."

Hissing and scuffling sounds from the classroom animal habitats caught Prescott's attention. "I'll bet you that's Atom," Prescott said. "He's probably skulking around, trying to see if he can catch one of our pets and eat it. Have you noticed that all the classroom animals seem to hate him?"

"If you say so," Alberta said. She was pulling out an especially long strand of artificial mucus.

"Clearly, I'll have to handle this myself," Prescott said. He crouched down and started to make his way toward the animal cages.

In the back of the classroom, Prescott peeked through the first habitat, an iguana tank. No Atom. He peered into the second habitat, a hamster cage. Atom was using a ruler to slide the food dish closer toward himself. The parrot poked his beak in for a bite, but the hamster charged at him. Atom backed away.

Prescott tracked Atom past the third habitat, a snake tank. The parrot gave it a wide berth.

No one noticed Prescott's silent sleuthing. All eyes were on Mr. Flask, who held up a large plastic beaker. "If the four lab groups will pour their cups of mucus in here, we'll have a quart — roughly equal to the amount you swallow each day."

"Yech!" Max gulped.

In the back of the classroom, Atom reached Wendy's cage and started jiggling the latch with his beak.

"I knew it!" Prescott leaped toward the bird. Atom squawked and flew over the boy's head. Prescott stumbled back and knocked over Max, who plowed headfirst into Mr. Flask — knocking the brimming beaker from his hands.

The students jumped away from the spreading puddle of mucus, but the professor ran right through it. He cornered Atom and carried him back to his perch.

Before he could stop himself, Prescott shouted out, "He didn't leave any foot-prints!"

The class turned to look at the professor. He stared back defiantly. "How could I leave footprints?" he said. "I walked *around* the mucus."

Mr. Flask was busy pulling desks away from the spreading puddle.

Prescott approached him. "I'm really sorry, Mr. Flask. I was just . . ." He stopped, unsure how to explain.

Mr. Flask smiled reassuringly. "Well, no use

crying over spilled mucus! This does look like a job for a cleaning professional, though. Alberta, could you find Mr. Klumpp and tell him we have a custodial emergency? Everybody else, recess! Let's give our bodies some exercise!"

CHAPTER 3

Mop vs. Mucus

Mr. Klumpp wheeled a cart full of mops into the science lab and surveyed the gooey mess. "Why can't these students just memorize facts from their textbooks? Flask teaches science like it's supposed to be fun!"

The custodian got down on his hands and knees and peered at the artificial mucus. "Looks viscous and moderately runny. I'll begin with a basic cellulose sponge mop." He pulled out the mop and checked its yellow head like a golfer inspecting a club. "This should do."

He plunged the mop into his pail and ran it through the slimy goo. The mop only spread the goo into a wider circle.

"Hmmm. Perhaps I've misjudged. Maybe an industrial-grade foam-scrubber mop would be more appropriate." Mr. Klumpp removed a blue-headed mop from his bag and again attacked the slimy goo. The circle got wider still.

The custodian looked at the goo with contempt. "So that's the way it's going to be, is it? Very well, you've forced my hand." Mr. Klumpp reached into his mop cart and pulled out a long parcel wrapped in brown paper. "Perhaps you've never experienced the unbridled power of a one hundred percent Egyptian cotton string mop." He unwound the paper and pulled out a red-handled mop that appeared to be topped with white dreadlocks. He lovingly untangled its thick strings with his fingers. "Gorgeous, you say? Yes, gorgeous, but deadly. She's never let me down."

Mr. Klumpp wet the mop and swirled it around in the pool of slime. Then he inspected the mop head. Goo clung to the wet strings. "Good job, girl. You show them who's boss." He wrung the mop head over the bucket. Water streamed back into the bucket, but the goo stayed on the mop. Mr. Klumpp frowned. He shook the mop, first gently, then harder and harder. Syrupy water drops dotted his face and clothing, but the goo clung stubbornly to the mop. He ran his hand along the mop head, and the goo came off on his fingers. He tried to shake it off his hands, spattering a whole row of seats with little yellow-gray dots. He clenched his fists and screamed.

While Mr. Klumpp battled the mucus inside, the sixth-grade science class hit the playground. Luis kicked a soccer ball around. Prescott joined him.

"Have you seen Atom?" Prescott asked Luis. "He's not with the professor."

Luis shrugged and bounced the ball off his knees. "Atom's probably perched in a tree. Maybe he's hunting for insects to eat or something. Don't some birds do that?"

"I bet he's back in the classroom hunting for a cute little white rodent," Prescott said. "We've got to save her!"

Luis moved around in circles. He practiced protecting the ball. "Don't worry. Even if Atom does want to eat Wendy, she's safe in her cage. Parrots don't break out of their own cages. It only follows that they can't break *into* another animal's cage, either."

"I've got to make sure," Prescott answered. "I don't trust that bird." He waved his hand and shouted. "Mr. Flask, may I go to the rest room?"

Mr. Flask nodded. Prescott took off like a flash across the playground. He bounded up the steps two at a time and raced down the hallway, slowing only when he encountered the scowling school secretary. Prescott burst into the science lab, barely noticing Mr. Klumpp. He ran straight to Wendy's cage and once again caught Atom fiddling with the latch.

Prescott reached for the nearest weapon — the ceramic popcorn bowl that had held Wendy's popcorn. He lifted it above Atom's feathered head. "Go ahead," he said. "Make my day."

"Don't shoot!" Atom raised his wings in a gesture of surrender.

Prescott wheeled around to face the custodian. "You heard him talk, too! Right, Mr. Klumpp?"

As soon as Prescott's eyes focused on the slime-covered Mr. Klumpp, he knew the custodian was in no mood to back up his story. Mr. Klumpp was sprawled in the puddle of goo, now a good three times its original size. A blob of slime sat atop his bald head like a bad toupee. Cradled in his lap was the mangled head of a red-handled string mop. The custodian looked like he was going to cry. Instead, he exploded.

"All I heard was the phantom laughter of this fiendish mess!" Mr. Klumpp held out the ragged mop in his slime-covered hands. "It has destroyed something dear to me!" He staggered to his feet. "But I will take my revenge. I shall return . . . with a wet vac!" He stormed out of the classroom.

Atom chuckled. "What a loser."

Prescott spun around, still holding the popcorn bowl. "I'm on to you, you . . . sentence-speaking rodent-eater."

Atom shrugged. "What can I say? I'm going through a carnivore stage. As for my talking, it must be your imagination!" He winked, then flew through the window and out into the school yard.

Prescott looked inside the mouse cage. Wendy peered cautiously out from under some wood chips. Cindy lounged in a corner, unconcerned. "You're safe this time," Prescott said. "But I wish you guys could bark, or something, to warn us the next time that parrot tries to get you."

Mr. Klumpp returned, pulling a huge canister on wheels. On the side it read HEAVY-DUTY WET-DRY VACUUM. He pulled out a handkerchief and wiped some of the gunk off his face. He turned to Prescott and held out the goopy cloth. "Your teacher is a mess just looking for a place to happen. What is this stuff, anyway?"

Prescott swallowed hard. "It's, uh, artificial mucus."

Mr. Klumpp's face turned beet red. "Artificial . . . *mucus*? Flask does this on purpose to make my life miserable!"

"Oh, no," Prescott started to object. But Mr. Klumpp clapped on a pair of sound-deadening earmuffs and revved up the wet vac. Prescott slipped out of the classroom as quickly as possible.

A few doors down the hall, Professor von Offel sat at his desk, dangling a scrap of white fabric from his fingertips. "You know, Atom, I really believe Flask is on to something this time. As he said, mucus really is a matter of life and death."

Atom flapped his wings impatiently. "Could you wiggle that fabric a little more energetically? I'm trying to sharpen my mouse-catching abilities here. She's going to be a moving target, remember?"

"Oh, yes." The professor flicked the scrap lazily a few times. "You know, tomorrow is hot dog day in the school cafeteria. Why not just fly by and scoop a hot dog off a kinder-gartner's plate or something? You could prac-tice being a predator that way."

Atom squawked. "Cafeteria food? Are you kidding me? I have my health to think about."

"I *was* thinking about your health," the pro-fessor said. "After all, hot dogs don't have teeth and claws."

"No teeth and claws?" Atom asked. "When was the last time you had a cafeteria hot dog?

Let's talk about something more appetizing. I believe you mentioned mucus. That qualifies."

The professor nodded. "I've had a brilliant flash of inspiration. Mucus is essential to life, as Flask said. So no doubt the application of extra mucus can help bring me fully back to life."

Atom shook his head. "You got this crazy idea from listening to Flask's straightforward, scientific lecture? You are a true von Offel."

"The original," the professor said. "I think a quart of mucus will do, don't you? This afternoon we'll buy the ingredients, plus a turkey baster."

Atom shuddered.

After school, Prescott hesitated outside of the science lab. "You want Wendy to be safe," he said aloud to himself. "So you have to warn Mr. Flask about Atom.

"Point taken," he answered himself. "But what am I going to do, tell him what Atom said about his 'carnivore stage'? Mr. Flask would never believe me!

"Don't even think about chickening out!" Prescott continued. "Just march in there and start talking."

Prescott took a deep breath and reached for the knob. Just then, the door swung open. The boy jumped a foot into the air.

"Hey, Prescott," Mr. Flask said. "Can I help you? I was just going to thank Mr. Klumpp for that great cleaning job. Maybe I'll give him a list of the ingredients for artificial mucus as well. It actually gave the floor a nice shine."

"It's about Wendy," Prescott began. "Actually, it's about Atom and Wendy."

Mr. Flask looked puzzled. "What does the professor's bird have to do with my mouse?"

"This may sound crazy, but yesterday I heard Atom calling Wendy 'fast food.' Then *twice* this afternoon I caught him trying to open her cage. He's out to catch and eat Wendy."

Mr. Flask laughed. "I'm sure you're giving that parrot too much credit. A student probably said something about fast food, and Atom repeated it. Anyway, parrots will eat meat if you offer it to them, but they aren't hunters. I appreciate your concern, but I'm sure Wendy is safe."

Prescott still looked agitated.

"Look," Mr. Flask said. "If you're that worried, I'll take Wendy home with me tonight. That way I can keep an eye on her. I'll bring her back in the morning, okay? You can feed her for me."

Before he went to sleep that evening, Mr. Flask made his nighttime tour of his cages and tanks. He noted with satisfaction that the nocturnal animals were starting to wake up. He left food for each of them. Mr. Flask also checked on Wendy, who was curled up in her cage, tired after a full day of exercise. Suddenly, something caught his eye. On the dusty windowsill, inches from Wendy's cage, were a set of medium-sized clawprints. Mr.

Flask looked across the lawn to Professor von Offel's house. He saw Atom, perched on a windowsill, staring back at him. "Could he have —?" Mr. Flask asked himself. "Nah-hhh." Even so, Mr. Flask closed the window before he turned out the light.

CHAPTER 4

"Where's That Turkey Baster?"

The three lab assistants huddled outside the school in the early morning chill, waiting for Mr. Flask.

"What are you guys going to wear to the costume dance?" Alberta asked.

Prescott bit his lip. "I haven't really thought about it yet."

Luis yawned. "Me, either."

"It's only two days away!" Alberta said.

"Well, what are *you* going to wear?" Luis

asked. "In fact, what did you two wear to last year's costume dance?"

"I made a very detailed robot costume," Alberta said. "I wore a box covered with aluminum foil and all kinds of knobs and dials. I had a hat cut out of a plastic milk jug, and I even had silvery tubing on my arms and legs."

Luis made a face. "Sounds hard to dance in."

"Well, I couldn't really dance at all," Alberta admitted. "But it was pretty fun just standing around in my costume."

"And you?" Luis asked Prescott.

Prescott cringed. "Well, I waited until the last moment, so I only had time to cut two eyeholes in a sheet and go as a ghost. "

"Oh, I remember that," Luis said. "Wasn't it a *flowered* sheet?"

Prescott looked sheepish. "Like I said, it was pretty last minute."

"This year, maybe we should work on something together," Alberta said.

"Yeah, theme costumes," said Prescott.

Luis looked at his two friends. He shook his head. "This is against my better judgment, but count me in. Let's meet after school and start brainstorming."

Just then, a shiny red car pulled up. Heather Patterson hopped out of the passenger side, carrying a stack of books and Cindy's cage.

Prescott blushed. "It's Heather Patterson."

"Wow, what's Heather Patterson doing here?" Luis asked.

Alberta rolled her eyes. "She goes to school with us, remember?"

"I wonder what Heather will wear to the costume dance?" Luis said.

Alberta rolled her eyes. "Duh! She'll wear her cheerleading outfit, just like last year . . . and every other year."

Alberta's critical tone brought Luis back to his senses. "Well, at least we can be pretty sure she's smart enough to wear something she can dance in!" he said.

Alberta turned toward the approaching figure. "Hello, Heather. I didn't know you'd volunteered for early morning animal care."

Heather didn't answer, she was too distracted. She actually looked less than perfect this morning. Her hair was hastily combed, and the circles under her eyes suggested she hadn't slept well.

"Is Mr. Flask here yet?" Heather asked.

"He should be here any minute," Luis assured her. "Is something wrong?"

Heather held up the cage. "I'm worried about Cindy. She won't eat anything — or at least not anything that's good for her. She completely refused both steamed zucchini and granola at dinner last night. Then after I went to bed, she broke out of her cage and went on a high-calorie rampage. This morning, we found an empty Twinkie wrapper on the counter. It was completely licked clean!"

Prescott shook his head sympathetically. "Wow, that's harsh."

Heather nodded dramatically. "I thought

maybe she had run away for good, but my mother found her lounging in the sugar bowl. I put this new exercise wheel in her cage, but she ignored it. In desperation, I tried to get her to at least do some yoga stretches, but she wouldn't lift a paw. She just sits there."

"Maybe the school nurse could see her," Luis suggested.

Mr. Flask arrived, holding Wendy's cage. He smiled, "Oh, good. Wendy and Cindy can do their morning aerobics together."

Heather sniffled. "Mr. Flask, something is terribly wrong with Cindy."

Mr. Flask peered into the cage. The gray mouse was stretched out on her back, a lazy smile on her furry face. "What seems to be the trouble?" Mr. Flask asked.

"She'll only eat junk food, and she won't exercise," Heather said.

"Hmmmmm." Mr. Flask unlocked the front door and led the way to the science lab. "Mice aren't known for being picky eaters. But we humans, at least, do seem to have a built-in preference for sweet and fatty foods. It probably helped our ancestors pick high-calorie foods, which would have been important for survival when food was scarce. Maybe mice have the same preference. I predict that if Cindy couldn't get to junk food, then she would be content to eat the same healthy foods that Wendy has been eating." Mr. Flask opened the door to the science lab and flicked on the lights. "Had she been eating a lot of junk food before this?"

"I certainly haven't been feeding it to her!" Heather said. "I don't touch the stuff myself. But Cindy seems to be really good at escaping from her cage. She's able to sniff junk food out, however well hidden."

"Mice do use smell to find food," Mr. Flask confirmed.

"Okay, this calls for direct action," Heather said. "From this moment forward, Cindy will never go unguarded. I'll only take her out of her cage to exercise. And I'll double-check to make sure that her cage door is latched whenever she's inside."

"Poor Cindy," Alberta muttered under her breath.

Several hours later, Professor von Offel opened the science lab door a crack and peeked inside.

"Excellent! They must all be at lunch. Come, Atom. We have just enough time to mix up a quart of mucus."

Atom flew in behind him, carrying a plastic grocery bag in his claws. "You're really going to go through with this, aren't you? I'll say one thing for you: You don't let common sense get in the way of any of your inspirations."

The professor filled a large beaker half full of hot water. Atom ripped open the gelatin packets with his beak. The professor stirred the powder into the water, then added the corn syrup.

"Now, for the moment of glory!" The professor plunged his hand into the beaker and pulled out a long, thick strand of goo. Syrupy water ran down his arm. "Where's that turkey baster?"

Atom held the utensil in one claw. "I can't believe you can even use one of these things in front of me. I'm a bird, remember? Basting is against our principles."

"This isn't about you," the professor said. "It's about me." He filled the turkey baster with artificial mucus and threw back his head. "Don't just sit on your tail feathers! Help me squirt this into each nostril!"

Prescott caught up with Mr. Flask outside the staff dining room. They walked toward the science lab. "Do you mind if I check on Wendy before my next class?" Prescott asked. "I didn't see Professor von Offel and Atom at lunch, and I just wanted to make sure —"

"Come to think of it, they weren't there, were they?" Mr. Flask said. "You're welcome to check. Of course, if I thought my mouse was in any danger, I wouldn't leave her in the lab."

They passed a long line leading to the boys' bathroom.

"You guys all right?" Mr. Flask asked.

The boys nodded queasily.

"It's like that every hot dog day," Prescott said after they turned the corner. "I swear by bag lun — whoa!" Prescott's feet flew out from under him. Mr. Flask acted quickly, grabbing Prescott's wrists and hauling him back upright.

Prescott steadied himself against the wall. Mr. Flask squatted down and touched the slippery floor experimentally.

"What is that stuff?" Prescott asked. "It almost looks like —"

"Artificial mucus," Mr. Flask confirmed. He stood up and looked down the hall. A foot-wide path of goop stretched to the door of the science lab. "Maybe Mr. Klumpp decided to condition the floors with it after all. He should probably go ahead and mop it up now, though."

Mr. Flask opened the door to the lab. A slimy beaker was tipped over onto his desk. Patches of artificial mucus dotted the floor and desks. A blob on the ceiling was dripping slowly.

"This doesn't look like Mr. Klumpp's work," Prescott said.

Mr. Flask nodded. "Well, at least this proves someone was paying attention in class yesterday." He smiled and tossed Prescott a sponge. "That's all we teachers ask."

They worked quickly and got the mess under control. As Mr. Flask finished scrubbing the blob off the ceiling, Prescott went back to check on Wendy.

"Uh-oh," Prescott said. "You better come have a look."

Just inside the door of the mouse cage was a puddle of artificial mucus. Wendy was running in her exercise wheel, ignoring it. But Cindy was hungrily lapping it up.

Prescott made a face.

"Well, it can't really hurt her," Mr. Flask said. "But it's certainly not health food, either." He unlatched the cage and wiped up the puddle. Cindy skittered angrily away.

The bell rang for sixth-grade science. The professor stumbled through the door, clutching a large wad of tissues. Atom flew behind him, a tissue box in his claws.

"Mr. Fla-ask!" Max's hand shot into the air. "I have a note from my mother."

Mr. Flask took the piece of paper. He read it to himself and then read it aloud. "Please excuse Max from before-school animal care. His circadian rhythms are very delicately balanced, so his sleep schedule may not be disturbed. Please allow him to earn extra credit some other way."

"Circadian rhythms — what does that mean?" Prescott asked.

"It means that he'd be tired if he got up early, just like the rest of us," Luis said.

Mr. Flask suppressed a laugh. "Circadian

rhythms are the cycles your body goes through during a 24-hour time period," he explained. "The most common example is that you feel sleepy at night and wakeful during the day. Scientists think the feeling of sleepiness comes from a chemical called melatonin. At night, our pineal gland pumps melatonin into our bloodstream, and we feel sleepy. When the sun comes up, the light triggers our brain to tell the pineal gland to stop pumping melatonin. That makes us feel more wakeful."

Prescott raised his hand. "Is that why I have a hard time getting up before sunrise? Or on a cloudy day?"

Mr. Flask nodded. "That's probably part of it. Circadian rhythms are a hot science topic right now. Scientists called *chronobiologists* are busy studying all of the changes our bodies go through during the day. For instance, your body temperature rises during the day and falls at night. Your handgrip is stronger in the afternoon than it is in the morning. Even your ability to remember things changes over the day."

In the back of the class, Professor von Offel scowled. "Flask, it zounds as dough you're zaying the huban body cad read a clock." He blew his nose loudly into a tissue and tossed it aside. Atom handed him a new one.

"Certainly not a clock on the wall, Professor," Mr. Flask said. "But our bodies do have their own internal clocks."

Alberta raised her hand. "I usually wake up just before my alarm goes off. And I wake up at the same time on Saturday, when my alarm isn't even set."

"Great example," Mr. Flask said.

Sean's hand shot up. "Every time they change the clock for Daylight Savings Time, it takes my body a week to get used to my new bedtime."

"Another great example." Mr. Flask beamed.

Max sniffed stubbornly. "I can't perform at my best when my circadian rhythms are disrupted. I need a different opportunity for extra credit."

"You're in luck, Max!" Mr. Flask walked over to a poster advertising the costume dance. "In order to promote the dance — and science — I'll give extra credit to anyone who wears a costume relating to our science unit on the human body. You can present your costumes during class on Friday."

Sean leaned toward Max. "You should dress like melatonin, because you sure put me to sleep." He laughed at his own joke, then discreetly reached into a paper bag near the foot of his desk. Suddenly, he jumped out of his chair. "Mr. Flask! There's something alive — and hairy — in my bag of candy!"

Mr. Flask approached the bag and gingerly lifted it up. Something inside squirmed and shuffled as the teacher carried the bag to the lab sink. The class gathered around. He set the bag in the bottom of the sink. Then he gently tipped it over. Out slid two half-eaten candy bars, a box of red hots, an open bag of cheese puffs, and a little gray mouse. Cindy held a cheese puff between her paws.

"Cindy!" Heather wailed. "How did you —? I tied the cage door shut with a piece of string!" Heather ran over to the cage. The door was open, and Wendy cowered in the far corner.

Prescott looked over at Atom. A piece of string dangled from his beak. "Atom untied the string!" he blurted. He edged closer to Mr. Flask and said more quietly, "I told you that bird wanted to eat Wendy."

The professor snapped the string out of Atom's mouth. He blew his nose noisily. Then he turned toward the class and shaped his mouth into a smile. "Surely you children know that birds gather bits of twig, hair, and string for their nests. Atom must have seen the string on the floor and picked it up. Bird behavior is largely controlled by instinct, after all."

Heather retrieved the string from the professor. After a withering look at Atom, she carried Cindy over to the cage and slipped her inside. She shut the door firmly and tied the string into a series of knots around the latch. "That better hold her," she muttered.

After science class, the professor grabbed hold of Atom and hurried off to his office. He slammed the office door behind him. "That scrawny little mouse can't be worth all the trouble you're causing!" said the professor.

"At this point, it's a matter of predator honor," Atom said. "I'll get her, just wait and see."

Professor von Offel blew his nose with a honk.

"So, feeling any more corporeal?" Atom asked.

The professor pulled a hand mirror out of his desk and checked for his image. He shook his head. "Still no reflection. I can't imagine what went wrong."

"Let me throw out a few possibilities," Atom said. "Number one, your idea had absolutely no foundation in science."

The professor looked offended. "I researched it with the same care I always do," he said.

"My point exactly," Atom replied. "Number two, a quart of liquid is a lot for any human body to absorb at one time. Don't you ever think of starting small?"

The professor's eyes blazed. "On the contrary, I don't think I went far enough!"

Atom covered his eyes with a wing. "You're completely unfazed by this whole incident. You almost gagged yourself to a second death in the science lab!"

The professor sniffed. "A mere setback."

"Well, it's a good thing I learned the Heimlich maneuver in the circus," Atom said. "I wonder how Flask got that mucus off the ceiling. Anyway, even if you don't care about *dying*, how about the possibility of being thrown out of Einstein Elementary? You're here with the principal's approval, after all. I can't imagine what she thought when she ran into us in the hallway."

"Anyone with a common cold produces extra mucus," the professor said.

"It was dripping off your chin!" Atom replied. "I'm surprised she didn't throw you out on the spot, just as a health code violation."

"This place is full of snot-nosed brats," the professor said. "She probably didn't even notice."

Atom shook his head in wonder. "You make denial an art form," he said.

While parrot and professor were bickering in the office, the lab assistants were brainstorming in the library. Alberta flipped through a book about human anatomy. "Okay," she said. "We need three excellent and related costumes having to do with the human body."

"All of them relatively easy to make," Prescott added.

"And none of them too bulky to dance in," Luis insisted.

Alberta nodded. "Anybody have any ideas?"

Prescott bit his lower lip in concentration. Luis stared up at the ceiling. The room was silent.

Alberta held up the book. "Okay, here are those three little bones in the middle ear — the hammer, the anvil, and the stirrup."

Prescott leaned over for a closer look. "I don't know. That hammer looks more like an ice cream cone, and the anvil looks like a high-heeled shoe."

Luis shook his head. "No way."

More silence.

Alberta spoke up again. "It says here that the brain has three main parts — the cerebral hemispheres, the cerebellum, and the brain stem."

"How could we dress up like the parts of

the brain?" Prescott asked. He reached for the anatomy book.

Alberta thought for a moment. "Well, we could all dress in gray sweat suits, to match the color of the brain. Then we could each carry something that is related to what our part of the brain controls, like breathing or balance or speech."

Luis was unimpressed. "Gray sweat suits?"

"Hey, let's hear your ideas," Alberta objected.

"Wait, I have one." Prescott held up a page. "There are three kinds of blood cells. Red blood cells carry oxygen. Alberta, you could wear your red gymnastics unitard and carry a white balloon to represent the oxygen. Then there are white blood cells, which fight disease. Luis, you could wear your white fencing outfit. That leaves platelets, the last kind of cell, for me. They help stop bleeding. I guess I could be covered with Band-Aids, or something."

"Don't you guys want people *outside* of science class to know what we're dressed as?" Luis asked. "If they see us in those costumes, they'll think we're a circus performer, a swashbuckler, and an accident-prone klutz. They won't get it. We need something cool, like my cousin's costume last year. Carlos wore this incredible glow-in-the-dark skeleton costume to his school dance. He said that when he moved it looked so eerie that it freaked everyone out. That's *my* idea of a costume."

Alberta smiled. "A skeleton definitely relates to our human body unit — in fact, it's the whole skeletal system."

"What if we each dressed as a different body system?" Prescott suggested. "I've got tons of old aquarium tubing at home. Maybe I could make a circulatory system costume — you know, the heart, veins, and arteries."

"I could take the nervous system — the brain, spinal cord, and nerves," Alberta said.

"You always wanted to be the brains of this group," Luis joked.

Alberta laughed. "As a matter of fact, I won

the brainy award in science two years ago, remember? The prize was a painter's cap that showed the brain. That's a good start on my costume."

Luis smiled. "Then I could borrow Carlos's skeleton costume — and dance until my bones rattle."

CHAPTER 5

A Scrumptious Spinal Column

Prescott stopped by the science lab after lunch.

"Watch your step," Mr. Flask said. "I'm letting the mice run around loose for a few minutes. Exercise is supposed to be fun, and I figure the wheel might get a little old sometimes."

"Aren't you afraid they'll run away?" Prescott asked.

"Wendy always comes back for her lunch,"

Mr. Flask said. "Cindy never goes farther than Sean's desk. I guess he drops a lot of crumbs."

"I brought something for Wendy," Prescott said. He produced a large bell with a button on top.

"The lunch monitor's bell?" Mr. Flask asked.

Prescott nodded. "I borrowed it until lunch tomorrow. I thought we could put it inside Wendy's cage. Then, if she wants to get our attention for any reason, she can press the button."

"She'll be the only mouse in town with a way to call room service," Mr. Flask joked.

"Well, it would be only for emergencies," Prescott said.

Mr. Flask's expression became serious. "Oh, this is because of Atom. You're still worried that he's after her, aren't you?"

Prescott blushed a little. "It's just that mice don't growl, or bark, or even meow. And she certainly can't fight. She needs *some* kind of defense against being eaten. I mean, what do mice do in the wild?"

"They run and hide," Mr. Flask said. "For a small animal like a mouse, that's the best defense."

"That doesn't work so well in a cage," Prescott replied.

"That's true," Mr. Flask said. "Okay, we'll try it. Of course, ringing a bell for help isn't a natural mouse behavior. It seems like it would take time for Wendy to learn it. But then, she's no ordinary mouse."

The rest of the science class trooped in.

"Red licorice and marshmallows?" Sean said as he passed Mr. Flask's desk. "Science class just keeps getting better and better."

"Say that again when the professor comes in," Alberta told him. "We have to keep reminding him what a great teacher Mr. Flask is."

Sean smiled. "I'll say it again for a candy bar."

"I'm not going to bribe you to tell the truth!" Alberta replied.

The bell rang, and the professor sailed into class with Atom in his wake.

"I agree, Sean," Alberta said loudly. "Mr. Flask's class *does* keep getting better and better."

"Why, thank you, Sean!" Mr. Flask walked to the front of the class. "I assume this has something to do with the marshmallows?"

"And the licorice," Sean said.

"Did you notice the mini rice cakes?" Mr. Flask asked.

"Yes, but I figured those were mouse food," Sean said. "I still don't understand how people can eat them."

Mr. Flask laughed. "What if I told you they were model vertebrae — the bones in your spinal column?" He picked up the marshmallows. "These are the model discs, which are made of squishy cartilage. And the licorice is a model spinal cord. Still hungry?"

"Of course!" Sean said.

"Then your lab group can do the Edible Spinal Column activity," Mr. Flask replied.

"Yes!" Sean raised a triumphant fist in the air.

"I'll have to watch that," Alberta whispered to Luis and Prescott. "Maybe I could use it in my nervous system costume."

"Prescott's group will do the Intestinal Squeeze."

"Intestinal squeeze?" Luis whispered back. "Sounds like what I'd get if I ate licorice, rice cakes, and marshmallows together."

"Alberta's group will do some vision tests, including a blind-spot test," Mr. Flask continued. "And Luis's group will make some model lungs."

As the groups gathered their materials, Mr. Klumpp stalked in. He was carrying a clipboard and wearing a tan safari vest, each of its seven pockets full. "I'm here to inspect the classroom habitats," he announced.

"Of course," Mr. Flask replied. "I'm sure you'll be happy with what you find."

"We'll just see about that." Mr. Klumpp stomped to the back of the classroom.

The lab groups settled down to their activities.

Mr. Klumpp started with the iguana tank. He plucked a measuring tape out of one pocket and checked the tank's length, width, and height. He pulled a calculator out of a second pocket and punched in some numbers. He checked the result against a book that he removed from a third pocket. He looked disappointed by what he found. "So the tank is of adequate size," he muttered. "That's one mark in your favor."

The custodian fished a thermometer out of a fourth pocket and lowered it into the tank. He produced a vial of pH indicator paper from a fifth pocket. He dipped one of the papers into the iguana's water bowl. "Hmmmph!" he muttered. "Normal pH."

Mr. Klumpp picked up the iguana's food dish and sniffed it. He drew a magnifying glass from a sixth pocket and inspected the food. Then he tasted some experimentally. "Fresh."

He checked his thermometer. "Within the acceptable range."

Finally, he slipped a white glove out of a seventh pocket and pushed his hand into it. He rubbed his gloved finger along one wall of the tank. He inspected the glove for soil. "Spotless."

Mr. Klumpp scowled as he scribbled notes on his clipboard.

Mr. Flask approached him. "Can I do anything to help?"

"Don't get cocky just because your iguana tank passed inspection!" Mr. Klumpp replied. "I still have ten more habitats to go."

Across the room, Sean, Max, and Heather were pushing short pieces of plastic straw through mini rice cakes.

"Stop eating the marshmallows, Sean," Heather said. "We need twenty-six discs for our model."

"So, we can have a shorter spine," Sean replied. He pointed to Max. "We could make a model of his spine. If a normal spine has twenty-six discs, his peewee spine probably only has fifteen or sixteen."

"Is that true, Mr. Flask?" Max called to Mr. Flask. "Do short people have fewer bones and discs in their spinal columns?"

Mr. Flask shook his head. "A kindergartner has the same number of spinal bones and discs as an NBA center. They grow with us."

Max turned to Sean. "So stop eating my discs!"

Mr. Klumpp finished measuring the snake tank, then peered nervously inside. "I'll give this tank a passing mark," he announced. "It looks clean enough from the outside."

"Those red rat snakes are as gentle as kittens." Mr. Flask walked back and lifted the lid. "If you like, though, I'll hold them while you inspect their habitat." The red-and-orange snakes curled around Mr. Flask's wrists. One tried to slither up his sleeve. He gently removed it with a laugh. "That tickles! I know you're looking for somewhere warm, but you'll be back in your tank in a moment."

Mr. Klumpp was staring at Mr. Flask, his eyes wide.

"Won't they?" Mr. Flask asked him.

Mr. Klumpp shook himself. He slipped on his white glove and hastily wiped the glass. "Looks fine," he said. "Please . . . that is, you may put them back now."

Prescott smiled to himself, then looked back down at his group's project. "We're supposed to pass this tennis ball though this panty-hose leg. We have to squeeze it through with our hands, kind of like squeezing the last bit of toothpaste out of a tube. The lab sheet says that this models peri, uh, *peristalsis*. That's the squeezing action of the muscles along the digestive tract."

The group stretched out the panty-hose leg. Prescott took the first turn squeezing the tennis ball through.

Mr. Klumpp walked over. "That's a very inefficient way of removing that tennis ball," he said. "Luckily, I specialize in having the right tool for the job." He plucked a pair of scissors out of a holster at his belt.

Snip! Prescott watched the tennis ball

bounce away, then looked at the two pieces of panty hose hanging limply. "Uh, thanks."

"Don't mention it," Mr. Klumpp said. He turned back to his inspection.

Atom sat atop the next habitat, the lizard tank. He tracked the little reptiles through the screened lid.

Mr. Klumpp frowned. "This parrot is consistently uncaged. I see no food for him to eat, no water for him to drink, no newspaper for him to, um, *utilize*. I'm sure that's some kind of violation!" He pulled out his book and began flipping through the pages.

Professor von Offel walked over and calmly picked Atom up. He turned to Mr. Klumpp. "Atom is *not* a classroom pet."

"Awk! Too bad, loser! Awk!" Atom squawked.

The professor flinched, then bared his teeth in a smile. "When you expose a parrot to a class of sixth graders, you never know what kind of language he'll pick up." He stalked away.

Mr. Klumpp inspected the lizard tank, then

moved on to the mouse cage. "Why is this door tied with string?" he demanded.

Heather rushed back to the cage. "One of the mice keeps escaping," she explained. "I've had to tie the door shut to keep her from opening it."

"I'm sure this is a fire code violation!" Mr. Klumpp replied. "How would you evacuate her if this classroom became a fiery inferno?"

Heather looked around, confused. "I suppose I'd carry her cage."

"There are eleven cages here!" Mr. Klumpp interrupted. "Could you carry them all?"

"I guess not," Heather said. "But other students could help."

"How can you be so sure?" Mr. Klumpp demanded. "You never know what will happen in an emergency. Do you really want to leave the lives of these mice to chance?"

Heather's mouth hung open. She was used to getting her own way without any argument. And this argument didn't even make sense.

Mr. Klumpp unholstered his scissors and snipped away the string.

"But she'll get out," Heather protested.

"It's that or risk having her trapped in the roaring flames!" Mr. Klumpp insisted.

Heather returned to her desk, stunned.

Sean was slurping up a long strand of red licorice.

"Leave some for the spinal cord!" Max said.

"Cut it out!" Heather snapped a piece of licorice away from Sean and began stringing the model together.

Mr. Klumpp gave the last habitat his white-glove test. He stared at the finger of his glove, still totally clean, and sighed.

Mr. Flask approached. "Do we meet with your approval?" he asked.

"I'll be back next week for another inspection!" Mr. Klumpp replied. He started toward the door, but Alberta's lab group caught his attention. They were all holding index cards in front of their faces. It looked like some kind of vision test. After his bad experience with the optical illusions unit, the custodian knew he should just keep on walking. But he couldn't help himself. "What are you students doing?" he asked.

"We're finding our blind spots," Alberta replied. She held her card out to him. "Would you like to try?"

Mr. Klumpp felt a shiver run up his spine. "No!" he shouted, and started backing quickly toward the door. "That is, my doctor has ordered me to stay away from eye tests of all kinds. Besides, I'm confident that I don't even have a blind spot." He turned around, just in time to slam into the edge of the opened door. He stumbled and grabbed onto the doorknob to steady himself. Then he staggered into the hallway. "What a blow!" he said as he left. "I even hear bells ringing."

"Wendy!" Prescott yelled. He scrambled out of his seat and rushed back to the mouse cage. Atom was trying to squeeze his body through the small door. Wendy was frantically pressing the bell. Cindy was nowhere to be seen.

Prescott grabbed the parrot by the tail feathers and flung him across the room. "Are you okay, Wendy?" The mouse looked up at Prescott. Her eyes grew wide, and she began ringing the bell again. "Don't worry, he's g— Ow!" Prescott spun around and saw Atom flying across the room with a clump of hair in his beak. He rubbed his head, finding a small bald spot. Atom landed on the professor's desk.

The professor calmly removed Prescott's hair from Atom's beak. "Another fine example of bird instinct," he announced. He rubbed Prescott's hair between his fingers. "Atom chose a very soft sample — perfect for cushioning his nestlings."

"Nobody move until we find Cindy!" Heather was on her hands and knees, looking under desks. "Sean, check your candy bag!"

Sean looked, but shook his head. The whole class got down on the floor to search. Mr. Flask stepped carefully around the room, checking the high surfaces. Suddenly, some movement caught his eye.

"I think we caught her," Mr. Flask said. He lifted the edible spinal column into the air. Dangling helplessly from the end was a small gray mouse. Cindy had managed to get her mouth around a marshmallow, but she couldn't bite through it. Mr. Flask gently removed her from the model, and Heather snatched her up.

"I knew she would escape!" Heather returned her to the cage.

"Nobody would sell a cage that mice could open," Mr. Flask reasoned. He looked at Prescott. "Or that parrots could open, either. I know we've had a strange string of coincidences this week. But Mr. Klumpp must have forgotten to latch the cage." He shook his head. "That's the only plausible explanation."

"I warned you not to get caught," the professor said to Atom when they got back to his office after science class.

"And I wasn't!" Atom laughed. "Flask is a true scientist. He'd need proof before he'd believe that a parrot was hunting his mouse. And he'll never get it from me."

"You'll just have to control your impulses," the professor replied.

"Listen to you!" Atom said. "Aren't you the man who impulsively inhaled a quart of artificial mucus?"

"There was nothing impulsive about it," the professor replied. "If you thought with lightning speed like I do, all of your actions would seem rash as well."

Atom shook his head. "Who can argue with *that* logic?"

"As it turns out, my mucus experience was valuable research," the professor continued. "I've used it to develop a much grander plan. This one will make a quart of artificial mucus look like child's play."

"Which is exactly what artificial mucus was meant to be," Atom said.

"Perhaps," the professor replied. "But *I* will use it as a base for greater things."

Atom buried his head in one wing. The professor scooped Atom up and perched him on his shoulder. "It's time to gather supplies."

CHAPTER 6

Playing Dress-Up

Luis and Alberta sat on the steps in front of Einstein Elementary and looked across the empty parking lot.

Alberta hugged herself to ward off the early morning chill. "That is a cool skeleton costume," she told Luis. "But you must be chilled to the *bone*."

Luis smiled and shook his head. "You've got some *nerve*."

Alberta looked down at her nervous system

costume — a black unitard painted with feathery silver lines. She laughed.

"Here comes the *heart* of our group now." Luis gestured toward Prescott, who was making his way across the parking lot in his circulatory system costume. A red fabric heart was pinned to his black sweatshirt. Clear tubing led from his heart to his arms, legs, and hands. The artery tubes were strung with red yarn. The vein tubes were strung with blue.

"Nice costumes," Prescott said. "But do you think the animals will recognize us when we feed them? Maybe they'll be scared of us."

"I doubt it," Luis said. "A lot of animals recognize odors, and we smell the same as always."

"I don't," Alberta said. She turned to show off the string of mini rice cakes and marshmallows running down her back.

Just then, Mr. Flask rolled up on his bicycle. He was dressed in green surgeon's scrubs. He locked his bike and carried Wendy's cage up the steps.

Prescott reached for the cage. "How are you doing, girl?" he asked Wendy. The mouse sniffed the air cautiously.

Mr. Flask led them through the front door. "Wendy seems a little nervous this morning. We had kind of a strange night. I thought I heard voices under my window. I went out with a flashlight, though, and I didn't see evidence of anyone — not even footprints. When I checked on my animals, they all seemed a little on edge. Then, when I flicked off the lights, there was a sudden, loud beating of wings outside. It was kind of freaky, but I'm sure it was just some neighborhood bird." Mr. Flask unlocked the science lab.

"I can guess *which* neighborhood bird," Prescott whispered to Wendy. Mr. Flask carried her cage to the back of the room.

"Mr. Flask, can I leave my spine here until after school?" Alberta unhooked her string of marshmallows and mini rice cakes. "I'm afraid I'll crush it if I wear it all day."

"No problem," Mr. Flask said. "You might want to put it where Sean can't see it, though."

"I'll put it in back," Alberta said. "I've noticed he never goes near the mice."

Prescott poured some oatmeal in Wendy's food dish. "I have to return that bell at lunch today," he told the mouse. "But I'll find some other way to protect you, I promise." Wendy sniffed at the oatmeal, then dug in.

As the bell rang for sixth-grade science, the door opened to reveal a ghoulish white figure. A hush swept through the room. Then a parrot landed on the ghoul's shoulder.

"The professor dressed up in a costume?" Alberta whispered. "That shows some class — and a sense of humor."

"A ghost?" Luis said. He turned to Prescott. "I bet you think this proves your theory about him."

"Look at his feet," Prescott whispered as

the professor walked by. "Can't you see they don't quite touch the ground?"

The door swung open again. This time, a huge bear blundered into the classroom.

"May I help you?" Mr. Flask asked.

The bear lifted a paw and pushed his snout toward the ceiling, revealing a sweaty human face underneath.

"Mr. Klumpp? Wow, that's some costume," Mr. Flask said.

"Naturally, I dressed up for the dance." Mr. Klumpp looked offended. "We custodians always do what we can to promote school spirit!"

"Of course," Mr. Flask said.

"I just spotted a huge can of corn syrup out in the hallway — must be about five gallons altogether," Mr. Klumpp said. "Is that for one of your experiments?"

Mr. Flask shook his head. "Maybe the cafeteria is making some baked goods for the dance?"

Mr. Klumpp looked unconvinced. "If it's all the same to you, I'll just, uh, rest here for a little while."

"Please," Mr. Flask said. "There's a chair in the back. You're just in time to see some of my students' science costumes. Who wants to be first?"

Sean's hand shot up. Mr. Flask motioned him forward. Sean had on a long-sleeved T-shirt that was stuffed with fake muscles. A tank top over it read WWF. A flashy gold chain hung around his neck. He had given himself long sideburns using a black Magic Marker.

Sean pumped up his arms, a chocolate bar in each fist. He arched one eyebrow. "I'm the world-famous wrestler Rock Candy!" He gave Mr. Flask a high five.

"And your human body connection?" Mr. Flask asked.

"Muscles, of course." Sean showed off his bulging biceps.

Mr. Flask laughed and made a mark in his grade book. "Next?"

Max struggled forward, his trunk encased in a huge white sphere. The front of his costume had a blue circle with a smaller black circle inside it.

"I'm an eyeball," Max explained.

"Duh," Sean said.

"I can even dilate," Max said. He turned a dial on the side of his costume. The black pupil grew larger.

"Nice touch," Mr. Flask said. He wrote in his grade book.

"Eyeballs have to stay moist," Max said. "So I was going to slather my costume with artificial mucus."

There was a gagging sound from Mr. Klumpp's corner of the room. Max started to push his way back down the aisle. Students leaned away reflexively.

"But I couldn't find a single box of unflavored gelatin," Max continued. "My mom took me to five different stores! It was unbelievably unfair."

"That's odd," Mr. Flask said. "But it's probably just as well. There's such a thing as a costume that's too realistic."

"I'll be next!" Heather danced to the front of the class.

"A cheerleading costume — what a surprise!" Alberta whispered to Luis.

"I'm adrenaline," Heather announced. "You know, the chemical that spurs you into action in emergencies." She lifted up her pompoms and cheered, "Two, four, six, eight. Danger's coming, you can't wait. You have to either run or fight. It's time to move with all your might!"

The boys in the class broke into spontaneous applause. Alberta slapped her hand to her forehead.

"Very creative," Mr. Flask said. He wrote in the grade book. "Now, let's get our three lab assistants up here."

Luis and Prescott stood up.

"Wait," Alberta said. She hurried to the

back of the classroom. "Hey, someone moved it." She turned toward Professor von Offel. "Have you seen my spinal column model, Professor? It's made of marshmallows, mini rice cakes, and red licorice."

The professor shook his head dismissively.

Alberta turned toward the custodian. "Mr. Klumpp, have you — oh."

Mr. Klumpp looked down at the half-eaten string of marshmallows and mini rice cakes in his paws. He swallowed. "What did you say this was?"

"My model spinal column," Alberta said slowly. "Bones, cartilage, nerves . . ."

Mr. Klumpp turned a little green. He struggled to his feet and thrust the model at Alberta. "Excuse me," he said, and bolted out of the room.

Alberta walked slowly to the front of the room. Mr. Flask took the model from her.

"Don't worry," he said. "You can do some reconstructive surgery before the dance."

After school, Alberta returned to the science lab to restring her spinal column. Prescott was helping Wendy work out. He had used small blocks to build stairs for her to run up and down. Luis was stocking the other animals' cages with enough food for the weekend.

The door opened, and an eye, framed in a monocle, peered in.

"Professor von Offel?" Alberta asked. "If you're looking for Mr. Flask, he's setting up the sound system in the gym."

The professor looked annoyed. "I didn't expect to find anyone in here — that is, anyone besides your teacher."

"That would definitely be the case in most classrooms," Alberta said. "But Mr. Flask is such a fantastic teacher that we like to spend extra time here. From a student's perspective, I can tell you that that's very rare. Mr. Flask is really a special . . ."

"That's probably enough," Prescott whispered.

". . . teacher," Alberta finished. She paused. The professor stood and stared at the three lab assistants. "Would you like to come in and wait?" Alberta asked him.

"Perhaps that's best," the professor replied. He entered, dragging a cart with several large boxes on it. He pushed them to the back and took a seat at his desk. "Proceed with whatever you were doing," he said. "I suppose you won't be here for long? Don't let me keep you."

"It's almost like he's trying to get rid of us," Prescott whispered.

"All the more reason to stay," Luis whispered back. "Maybe we can learn a little more about him."

Alberta nodded.

"Professor, did you grow up here in Arcana?" Luis asked.

"Yes," he said.

Luis waited for him to offer other details, then prompted, "I bet it's changed a lot since you left."

"Yes."

"What's changed the most?" Luis asked.

"Youngsters," the professor answered. "They feel free to ask so many questions these days."

The lab assistants worked quietly for a moment. Then Alberta spoke up.

"Professor, have you ever read the scientific notebook of Johannes von Offel?"

The professor's eyes narrowed. "What makes you think that I have?"

"I just thought that since he's your ancestor . . ."

"Oh — of course. Where have they stashed it, anyway?" the professor asked. "I have some corrections to make."

"It's in the rare book room of the public library." Alberta looked puzzled. "But they practically keep it under lock and key. I can't imagine they'd let anyone write in it."

"Why would I write in it?" the professor asked.

"Well, the corrections you mentioned," Alberta said.

The professor was silent.

Alberta finished restringing her spinal cord. Luis closed up the last animal habitat.

Prescott returned Wendy to her cage. Cindy was curled up in the corner, her whiskers sticky with marshmallow. Prescott looped a combination padlock through the cage door and clicked it closed. "That should keep you safe," he whispered to Wendy. Then he turned to the professor. "That ghost costume you were wearing, where did you get that idea?"

"It was clever, wasn't it?" the professor said. "I'll tell you my secret. I simply cut two holes in an old sheet and slipped it over my head. I think it may become all the rage someday."

"Maybe so," Prescott said. "How did you get interested in ghosts, anyway?"

The professor frowned. "What makes you think I'm interested in ghosts? I never give them a second thought!"

"Do you *believe* in ghosts?" Prescott asked.

The professor stared at Prescott for a long

minute. Finally, he said, "Let's just say I've seen evidence they exist."

Prescott stared back. "What a coincidence. So have I."

The two stared at each other for a few seconds longer. Then the professor laughed harshly.

"You children look finished with your tasks," he said. "You may go now. I'm surprised young Flask allows you to be alone in the science lab with all of this dangerous equipment — Bunsen burners, glass beakers, and the like. This *is* where that equipment is, isn't it?"

Alberta nodded. The lab assistants gathered their belongings and went reluctantly to the door.

"No need to bother Mr. Flask, children," the professor said as they left.

As soon as they were outside, Luis said, "To the gym, right?"

Alberta and Prescott nodded.

They found Mr. Flask under the makeshift stage, splicing together color-coded wires.

"The professor's in the science lab," Alberta told him.

"Did he say what he wanted?" Mr. Flask asked.

"No," Prescott answered. "But I know he's up to no good. He seemed eager for us to leave."

Mr. Flask smiled. "He does seem kind of nervous around students. I'll try to stop by if I get a chance, but I have a lot to do before the dance begins."

"Should we go back and keep an eye on the professor?" Luis asked.

Mr. Flask shook his head. "If you guys are free, I know Principal Kepler could use your help with the decorations. That's more important. I mean, how much trouble can the professor get into in a sixth-grade science lab?"

CHAPTER 7

Superpowered Muscle-Regenerating Body Rub

Lucky for me, I learned to pick locks in the circus." Atom studied Prescott's combination lock. Wendy and Cindy were curled up in the far corner of the cage, both snoring softly. "It was one of my favorite acts. I was master magician and escape artist Harry Clawdini." He rocked back on his tail and flapped his wing tips. Then he grasped the knob and began turning it clockwise.

Professor von Offel shook a packet of unflavored gelatin into a beaker of steamy water. To his right was a complicated set of test tube racks, Bunsen burners, coils, and beakers. To his left was a stack of empty gelatin packets. A huge glass vat stood on the floor next to him. "Just get on with it," he told Atom. "I'm going to need your help."

"I'll be with you in under two minutes," Atom said. He found the first number of the combination and began turning the knob counterclockwise. "Speed was the point of my whole Clawdini act. They wrapped me in butcher paper, shut me in a padlocked cage, and slowly lowered me into a vat of water. I had two minutes to escape, or I'd drown." He found the second number and started turning the knob clockwise again. Cindy yawned and stretched. Her eyes focused on Atom for a moment, then closed sleepily.

"I'm sure the pressure was deadly." The professor began opening bottles of corn syrup. "Your story's certainly killing me."

"Without butcher paper to slow me down,"

Atom continued, "I should be into this cage in under a minute. That gives me another full minute to enjoy a leisurely mouse dinner. Then I'm all yours. Ah, here we go." He tugged gently on the lock, and the clasp opened with a quiet click.

The professor continued to open packet after packet of gelatin, while on the other side of the school, students streamed into the darkened gymnasium. The background music pounded a steady beat as Mr. Flask made last-minute adjustments to the sound system.

Sean was at the microphone, pumping up the crowd. "I want to see everyone out there having fun, or I'm going to have to get nasty on you." He showed off his fake biceps. The crowd went wild.

Mr. Flask turned from the sound system console and gave Sean a thumbs-up.

"Okay," Sean told the crowd. "Are you rhythm impaired? Did you wake up with two left feet? Help is on its way. There's a doctor in the house — Dr. Flask!"

The crowd broke into applause. Mr. Flask pulled on his operating room mask and waved.

"The doctor's sound system is guaranteed to cure whatever ails you!" Sean shouted. "For your first dose of dance medicine, one of my personal favorites."

Mr. Flask pushed some buttons, and the gymnasium filled with a pulsing rhythm. Flashing lights bounced off the growing crowd of dancers.

Mr. Klumpp stood on the sidelines, a push broom in his furry bear paws. Two fifth graders walked by in elaborate papier-mâché costumes of a sun and a moon. An orange piece of crepe paper — one of the sun's beams — detached and fluttered to the floor. The custodian grumpily swept it away.

Principal Kepler approached the lab assistants. She was dressed like a paleontologist, with a safari suit, a pith helmet, and a belt hung with excavation tools. She motioned for all three to join her on the dance floor. "You guys did a great job on the decorations," she shouted over the music. "Let's have a celebratory dance."

Back in the classroom, Atom wasn't celebrating — yet.

"Haven't you caught one yet?" the professor asked. He was strapping flasks into an electric agitator.

Atom hopped from desk to desk. "Mice are faster than I expected, and sneakier. Who knew mice could fake sleep? As soon as I opened the cage, the little rodents bolted."

"Did you think they would just put up their little paws and surrender?" the professor asked.

"That would have been nice," Atom replied.

"I thought you had an overwhelming urge to hunt," the professor said.

"I do," Atom said. "But my urge to eat is even more overwhelming. . . . Ah, there's the gray one."

Atom swooped down toward Cindy, claws extended. The gray mouse made a break for Mr. Flask's desk, but she was too slow. Atom trapped her tail with one claw and used the other to feed her, face first, into his beak. He worked her about halfway in, then — *ptooey* — spit her across the room. She hit the floor running.

"Yeee-uck!" Atom flapped over to the sink and turned on the faucet. He took a long drink. "That one tasted like a beef jerky, cotton candy, and orange jelly slice sandwich. I guess you really are what you eat." He wiped his beak with his wing. "This time, it's Wendy or nothing."

The professor unstrapped the flasks and poured the chemicals into the glass vat. "While you're over there putting a kink in the food chain, I'm setting new standards for genius. Aren't you even curious about my latest brainstorm?"

Atom sighed. He hopped over to the clear glass vat of green goo. "Is this Tex-Mex dipping sauce? Maybe Wendy would like to go for a swim."

"What you behold is my superpowered muscle-regenerating body rub, using a base of artificial mucus. It's absolutely guaranteed to build up my missing 35 percent."

Atom fluttered up and landed on the rim of the vat. The fumes immediately knocked his head back. "Whoa! What reeks?"

The professor smiled fondly. "That must be the skunk oil reacting with the injected bubbles of sewer gas. Powerful stuff, indeed. Now, let's put my plan into action."

"Not until I've had my appetizer," Atom said. "I have a feeling I shouldn't work with that stuff on an empty stomach."

"I'll give you two minutes, Clawdini," the professor said. "Then I'm getting out the butcher paper myself."

Atom hopped to the ground and walked the length of the classroom, peering under the columns of desks. He caught sight of Wendy hiding under Prescott's desk, but he kept walking as if he hadn't seen her. When he reached the last column, he flew across the classroom and dropped down right behind Prescott's chair. Wendy jumped straight in the air, then took off toward the front of the class. Atom scrambled after her.

Wendy was in better shape, but Atom had the advantage of longer legs. Just as he was about to pounce on her, Cindy appeared out of nowhere and threw herself between them. As the parrot tumbled over Cindy, she caught his chest feathers with her front claws. "Get — this — vermin — off — of — me!" Atom shouted, as they bounced across the floor.

The professor looked up, amused. He didn't notice Wendy skittering up his coat and into his pocket.

Atom and Cindy rolled to a halt, with the mouse on top. She got right in Atom's face and squeaked angrily. Then she hopped off and put her front paws on her hips.

"I guess she told you." The professor

laughed. "Now that she knows you won't eat her, she's fearless."

Atom shook his feathers. "She only beat me because I'm weakened from hunger. Things would be different if I'd had the brains to work for the Flasks instead of the von Offels. Then I wouldn't be so ill fed that a scrawny little white mouse was an irresistible feast!"

The professor scowled, then turned and wrestled the glass vat off the ground. "Just use your remaining strength to help me get to the gymnasium's weight room," he said.

Over in the gym, the party was really heating up.

"I have it on good authority that this next song is Dr. Kepler's favorite," Sean told the crowd. "It's an oldie, but it has a good beat. This is your chance to get on the principal's good side. Get out there and show her you can *disco*!"

Sean jumped from the stage and reached

for Dr. Kepler's hand. She laughed, and two of them danced away. Heather began a line of strutting students that snaked its way around the dance floor. The lab assistants joined in, dragging along Max, who had been sulking on the sidelines.

Nobody noticed two figures outside the weight room at the end of the long gymnasium.

"Push harder!" the professor ordered.

Atom leaned his head against the weight room door and flapped his wings frantically. "This is ridiculous," he said. "Anybody who can get through this door has no business lifting weights. It would be overkill."

The professor was straining under the weight of the vat. Finally, he shouted, "Coming through!" Using the vat as a battering ram, he busted the door open. Some of the green goo sloshed on the floor. The professor lowered the vat to the ground.

Working quickly, the professor loaded a dozen 25-pound weights onto a barbell. He stripped off his shirt and lay down on the bench under the weight. He gripped the bar with both hands and heaved. It didn't budge.

Music from the gymnasium resonated inside the weight room. Atom twitched his tail feathers. "I'm feeling the overpowering urge to shake my groove thang!"

The professor ignored him. "Begin the application!"

Atom dipped a wide paintbrush into the vat and slathered green goo all over the professor's arms and torso. As the preparation soaked into the professor's skin, a thick mist billowed up into the room and began seeping under the door. The professor strained. Very slowly, the barbell began to stir.

"It's working!" the professor said. "I can feel my muscle cells multiplying!"

Atom coughed. "Can you feel my beak disintegrating? I can't breathe in this stink."

"Keep slathering!" the professor replied. He

shut his eyes and tried to block out the sounds from the gym.

"Let's take a vote," Sean bellowed into the microphone. "Everyone who wants to 'party like it's *still* 1999' with Mr. Flask's music pick, shout out."

Mr. Flask held up a CD case for the crowd to see. The lab assistants screamed their support. Dr. Kepler let out a Tarzan yell.

"Impressive, Dr. K.!" Sean held up a hand. "Okay, everyone who wants to join me in the twenty-first century, shout out."

The gymnasium erupted in loud cheers.

"The people have spoken, Mr. Flask," Sean said.

Mr. Flask gave a good-natured sign of defeat. He pushed a few buttons, the music blared, and hundreds of costumed bodies resumed their gyrations.

Prescott bobbed closer to Alberta and Luis. He wrinkled his nose. "Do you smell something funny?"

❄ ❄ ❄

Atom balanced on the edge of the vat, the paintbrush in his beak. He leaned forward to dip the brush in the ointment. Between his claws, he saw the upside-down image of the professor's shirt, crumpled on the ground — with Wendy peeking out of the pocket.

He dropped the brush. "Lunchtime!" he crowed, and flew at Wendy.

"Don't stop!" the professor yelled. "I'm almost strong enough to lift this thing."

But Atom was locked on target. Wendy darted out of the pocket just in time, leaving Atom to untangle himself from the professor's shirt. She scampered up the professor's leg.

Atom tracked Wendy up the professor's body. She perched on his nose.

"Keep still!" Atom squawked. "I've almost got her!"

"No!" the professor yelled. Atom dive-bombed the professor's face. Just before he made contact, Wendy executed a perfect swan dive straight into the bucket of superpowered muscle-regenerating body rub.

Atom wrestled with the professor's nose for a moment before he realized the mouse was missing.

The professor sputtered angrily and knocked Atom to the floor.

Atom shook himself. Then he hopped on top of the barbell and looked around. Churning liquid in the vat caught his eye.

"Now I've got you!" He perched on the rim and leaned in. Suddenly, Wendy surfaced out of the green slime, her mouse muscles bulging from superexposure to the professor's ointment. She grabbed Atom by the tail feathers, twirled him effortlessly over her head, and launched him into the cinder block wall.

She jumped down onto the professor's chest and ran up his arm, adding her strength to his struggle with the 300-pound weight. Together, they hurled the barbell toward the ceiling. Its force cracked the plaster. The professor sprang up from the weight bench just in time to watch the barbell do a deadweight drop onto the glass vat.

The vat shattered, spraying the walls with glass. Dense white mist choked the room. Wendy paused to thumb her whiskered nose at the still-dazed Atom, then scrambled under the door to freedom. Gallons of foul-smelling liquid oozed after her and began spreading toward the dance floor.

CHAPTER 8

The Bear Bares His Underwear

S tink bomb!" yelled Mr. Klumpp. Swinging his push broom wildly at the approaching mist, he led a stampede to the other side of the gym.

Back in the weight room, the billowing mist reached the ceiling and triggered the smoke detector.

In every room of the gymnasium, the sprinkler system kicked on. Water poured from the ceiling. Mr. Flask swung into action, pulling the plug on the sound system. He jumped off the stage into the crowd. "Let's remain cool!" he shouted over the earsplitting alarm. "Find the fire exit nearest you. Walk, don't run toward it. Stay calm!"

"Can we help?" Alberta asked. The three lab assistants gathered around Mr. Flask.

Mr. Flask nodded. "I have to find out where that mist is coming from. Could you help those two to the exit?" He pointed to the two fifth graders dressed as the sun and moon. They were pinned to the floor, their water-soaked papier-mâché costumes rapidly lique-fying. The lab assistants surrounded them and pulled off slimy handful after slimy handful until the two fifth graders were free. Then they helped them to the exit.

Alberta pointed across the dance floor to Mr. Flask, who was disappearing into a misty corridor. "Let's follow Mr. Flask. He might need us."

Luis shook his head. "He asked us to help the other students get out."

"Just those two fifth graders, which we did," Alberta argued. "He didn't say we couldn't join him afterward."

"Maybe we should wait for the fire department," Prescott said.

"That's not smoke," Alberta said. "It's mist. And smelly as it is, it can't be poisonous because no one's been affected. I'm ninety-nine percent sure it's safe. As Luis says, Mr. Flask doesn't take unnecessary risks. And in case of that unsafe one percent, Mr. Flask will need us."

Luis nodded. Prescott threw up his hands. Alberta led the way toward the misty corridor.

Across the room, Mr. Klumpp was lying on his furry back. "I've fallen, and I can't get up," he groaned. He tried to right himself, but his bulky suit was too waterlogged. Finally, he sighed. "When duty calls, I must make any sacrifice needed to restore order. It's the custodian's creed." He heaved his paw behind his back and managed to catch his costume zipper. He writhed on the ground until he got the zipper down. Then he emerged from the pile of fur, dressed in nothing but his underwear.

Back in the weight room, the torrent of water from the sprinkler system had washed the goo off the professor's torso. He lifted one arm and experimentally thrust it through one wall.

"I told you it wouldn't work." Atom rubbed his head with his wing. He hadn't moved a feather from where Wendy threw him.

The professor shrugged. "This happens in science every now and again."

The lab assistants held hands as they made their way through the mist-filled corridor. With each step, they had to pry their feet out of the trail of green goop: *squelch, squelch, squelch.*

Luis held his hand out in front of him. He could barely see it. "I wonder if this is what the inside of a cloud looks like," he said.

"I don't know," Alberta answered. "But this stench reminds me of our fourth-grade field trip to the sewage treatment plant."

Prescott made a face. "Did you have to remind me? That's when I learned that in order to smell something, tiny pieces of it have to be inside your nose. I avoided the school bathrooms for a whole year after that!"

Luis sped up. "Shh! I think I just heard a door being opened ahead of us."

"And I hear a crashing sound behind us," Prescott added.

"Let's check it out," Alberta whispered.

Mr. Flask was surveying the weight room from outside the open door when the lab assistants caught up with him. The room had a wall-to-wall carpet of green goop and broken glass. The parrot lay dazed and unmoving in one corner. The professor sat, shirtless, on a weight bench, calmly wiping his brow with a sopping wet towel.

Abruptly, the alarm and sprinkler system switched off. The professor smiled with satisfaction and stood up.

Mr. Flask took a deep breath. "What happened here?"

The professor snorted. "I decided to do a little investigating of my own on your theories about physical fitness. While I was doing so, the smoke detector malfunctioned. "

There was a crashing and clanging in the hallway, and Mr. Klumpp pushed his way into the room. He was dressed in his underwear, and he was wearing garbage can lids on his feet like enormous beach sandals.

"I knew I'd find you at the bottom of this, Flask," the custodian fumed. "You probably thought you could throw me off your trail — standing on the stage in plain sight and playing innocent. But this slime has Flask written all over it! It's my business to know messes, and I would bet a ton of cleaning rags that this is some form of artificial muc —"

"Clearly, this is mildew," the professor cut him off. "Look, it's green. That proves it. I'm amazed that Dr. Kepler keeps you here, given the shabby condition of this weight room." The professor thrust his wet towel into the custodian's hands. "I'd suggest you get cleaning. If things are satisfactory on Monday, I'm sure that Flask and I will keep this little incident to ourselves." Professor von Offel picked up Atom, balanced the parrot on his shoulder, then walked to the door. "And for the love of all that's decent, man, put some clothes on!" He strode away.

Mr. Flask and his assistants never got a word in. They, too, headed out the door. Mr. Klumpp was left alone to fume.

"I've never seen anyone so angry," Prescott said as he, the other lab assistants, and Mr. Flask made their way back to the science lab.

"Mr. Klumpp is a very passionate man,"

Mr. Flask said. "I guess that's what makes him so good at what he does. I may need to talk to him about some of his more colorful expressions, though."

"I liked that one about the fleas of a thousand camels," Alberta said.

Mr. Flask opened the science lab door. Inside, the professor was humming tunelessly and returning science equipment to the cupboards. He turned and brushed off his hands. "Well, Flask, that's that. See you on Monday."

"Hey, look at this!" Prescott carried over the mouse cage. Wendy was inside the exercise wheel, spinning it so fast that sparks flew from both ends of the axle. "I guess all that exercise and healthy eating paid off."

At the sight of Wendy, Atom shuddered and cowered behind the professor's neck.

Inside the cage, Cindy held a marshmallow in her paws and stared at Wendy's performance. Suddenly, she looked down at her sugary treat and threw it over her shoulder. She headed straight for Wendy's food dish and began chowing down on carrot sticks. Prescott laughed. "Looks like you've got a health food convert, Mr. Flask."

"Let's check Wendy's maze time right now," Luis suggested.

Mr. Flask thought for a moment. "I've got to go back out and help Dr. Kepler close up the gym. Why don't you go find Heather and remind her to pick up Cindy and take her home for the weekend. Stop by my house around noon tomorrow, though, and we'll run the maze test then."

It was midnight by the time Mr. Flask and Dr. Kepler had a chance to sit down and rest.

"The students are safely home, and the mess is cleaned up, but this isn't over yet," Dr. Kepler said. "There's the matter of Professor von Offel."

Mr. Flask nodded. "Whenever anything bizarre happens, he always seems to be in the thick of it. And though we can't hold his family history against him —"

"It does make you wonder," Dr. Kepler agreed.

"The problem is, we have no direct evidence," Mr. Flask said.

"Spoken like a true scientist," Dr. Kepler said. "There's an even bigger problem, though. The professor is key to your winning the Vanguard Teacher Award, an award you definitely deserve."

Mr. Flask sighed.

"That settles it," Dr. Kepler said. "We'll hold off any action for now. Let's just stay on the lookout for any other unusual incidents."

"I have a feeling that's not going to be too difficult," Mr. Flask said.

Saturday morning the lab assistants gathered at Mr. Flask's house. The cardboard maze was already out on the front lawn. Mr.

Flask came out the door carrying Wendy's cage. The little white mouse was inside her exercise wheel, spinning wildly.

"Did you see Heather's face last night when she saw Cindy eating a carrot?" Alberta asked. "She was so ecstatic, I thought she was going to kiss you."

Prescott's eyes grew wide. "Really?"

Mr. Flask walked out holding a stopwatch in one hand and a package of cheese in the other.

Luis reached for the cheese, broke off a large chunk, and dropped it at the end of the maze. "That mouse is going to need some serious calories after all of this exercise."

"How did she get to be such a speed demon?" Alberta asked.

Mr. Flask shrugged. "Wendy hasn't been the same since the dance. Last night she broke out of her cage and raced around the house for hours. And when I say broke out, I mean the bars were actually bent open."

"Atom?" Prescott asked.

"There's no way. The windows were all

shut and locked." Mr. Flask held up the stopwatch. "Okay, I'm ready when Wendy is."

Prescott gently removed Wendy from her cage and held her over the starting block.

"Ready, set . . . go!" Mr. Flask clicked the stopwatch.

Wendy hit the ground running — directly into the maze's first cardboard wall. She flattened that wall, then the next, then the next, then the next. Using brute strength and her sense of smell, she plowed a straight path to the cheese.

"Six seconds!" Mr. Flask said.

Prescott picked Wendy up. "Great job, girl! That must be about a fourteen million percent improvement."

"*That* can't be true, can it?" Alberta asked.

Mr. Flask smiled. "Luckily, I'm not your math teacher."

"So, clearly, Wendy's fitness has improved," Luis said. "But did you learn anything about animal intelligence?"

Mr. Flask reached out and scratched Wendy's head fondly. "It's hard to say."

Suddenly, a flowerpot dropped from above, missing Wendy by inches. Prescott jumped back as it shattered at his feet. "Hey!" he shouted. The group looked up. Atom sat on a second-story windowsill, glaring down at Wendy.

"I don't know about you guys," Prescott said. "But I've learned just enough about animal intelligence to keep me on my toes."

Welcome to the World of
MAD SCIENCE!

The Mad Science Group has been providing live, interactive, exciting science experiences for children throughout the world for more than 12 years. Our goal is to provide children with fun, entertaining, and exciting activities that instill a clearer understanding of what science is really about and how it affects the world around them. Founded in Montreal, Canada, we currently have 125 locations throughout the world.

Our commitment to science education is demonstrated throughout this imaginative series that mixes hilarious fiction with factual information to show how science plays an important role in our daily lives. To add to the learning fun, we've also created exciting, accessible experiment logs so that children can bring the excitement of hands-on science right into their homes.

To discover more about Mad Science and how to bring our interactive science experience to your home or school, check out our website:

http://www.madscience.org

We spark the imagination and curiosity of children everywhere!